MYSTERY of the MIDNIGHT VISITORS

Written by Erica Frost

Illustrated by Ann Gamache

Troll Associates

Troll Associates, Mahwah, N.J.

Library of Congress Catalog Card Number: 78-18038
ISBN 0-89375-094-8

MYSTERY of the MIDNIGHT VISITORS

When Sarah Blake was eleven years old, her great-aunt Hester gave her a most wonderful present . . . a pane of glass for her bedroom window! The glass had been made by hand in England, far, far away. It was full of bumps and bubbles.

Sarah's bedroom was Rachel's bedroom and Robert's bedroom and Seth's bedroom and John's bedroom. But Sarah was the eldest, and the pane of glass was *hers*.

Sarah loved her wonderful window.
When she looked through the bumpy glass,
everything looked different. The apple tree

outside her window seemed to tremble. The
dark woods waved and shivered. Sunlight
ran over everything like wet, yellow paint.

Early one morning, Sarah jumped out of bed. She was happy and excited. It was the day for her trip into Boston with her father.

"Lucky you!" said Robert. "I wish I were going too."

"Next time," said Sarah. "Quick now! Tuck in your shirttail. You know that Pa does not like to be kept waiting."

The children hurried in for breakfast. The girls sat on one side of the table. The boys sat on the other.

Breakfast, on that early autumn morning, was warm milk and bread. The bread was freshly baked. Its good smell filled the cozy room.

The Blake family bowed their heads. Sarah's father said the blessing. Then he cut the bread and passed the thick slices around. Sarah's mother poured the milk. They ate in silence, for it was their custom.

   When breakfast was over, Rachel took
up her knitting. She was making a pair of
stockings for John. There were so many
things to finish before winter set in.
Stockings. Caps. Mittens. Mufflers.

Tomorrow, Sarah would be there to help.
But today, Rachel must work alone. Click!
Click! Click! The needles seemed to fly in her
fingers.

Robert and Seth helped their father load the wagon box. They loaded it with corn and wheat. John, the youngest, helped too. They hitched up Sam and Old Noah.

Sarah tied on her bonnet. She climbed
up on the seat, next to her father.

"I fixed some corn cakes and apple
cider," said mother. "I know you both. You
will be hungry as bears as soon as the wagon
rounds the bend."

Everybody laughed. Sarah kissed her mother goodbye. Then her father called to the team. The horses shook their heads and started up. They were on their way!

Two hours later, the wagon drove into the city of Boston.

What a busy city it was! Smoke rose up from hundreds of chimneys. Dogs barked. Chickens cackled. Roosters crowed. Gulls screeched as they flew in great circles and swooped down over the rooftops.

Fish peddlers pushed their barrows up and down the cobbled streets.

"Fish!" they called. "Cod! Halibut! Fresh oysters! Buy my fresh fish!"

Boys shouted to each other as they carried water from the town pump. Pigs ran through the streets looking for their breakfast.

Shipbuilders, shopkeepers, tailors, and tanners were busy at work. The city of Boston was awake and ready for business.

Sarah's father stopped their wagon at the miller's, and began to unload his sacks of corn and wheat.

"Good morrow, Jebediah," said Mr. Blake. "Fine morning, isn't it?"

"That it is," agreed the miller. "And a fine looking daughter you have there!"

Sarah smiled at the miller. She felt grown-up to be in the city of Boston with her father.

"How old are you, young lady?" asked the miller.

"Eleven years old, sir," answered Sarah.

"The same age as young Josh Tucker," said the miller. "Being neighbors, I suppose you've heard what happened."

"No, sir," said Sarah.

"What did happen, Jebediah?" asked Mr. Blake.

"Well," said the miller, who loved to tell a story, "seems like some Indians gave Missus Tucker quite a fright."

"What happened to her?" asked Sarah.

"Missus Tucker was setting her bread near the window to cool," said the miller. "She saw some Indians peering into the house. Old Joshua was nowhere in sight. So she turns to young Josh and says: 'Quick, boy! Go get your Pa's gun and close the shutters. There's Indians outside!' "

"Then what happened?" asked Sarah.

"Quiet, Sarah!" said her father. "Let the miller tell his story."

"Young Josh is a smart lad," continued the miller. " He looked out the window. The Indians looked friendly. 'It's all right,' he told his Ma. 'These Indians are our friends.' Then he opened the door, and asked them to come in."

"What happened then?" asked Sarah, forgetting her father's warning.

"Sure enough," said the miller. "The Indians had beads and spices and a new bow for young Josh. They were paying a proper visit. That's all. Missus Tucker gave them some milk and corn bread, and everything turned out fine. Thanks to young Josh, that is."

"Wasn't he scared?" asked Sarah.

"No," laughed the miller. "Not Josh Tucker. Scared is for girls and sissies. Young Josh Tucker is as brave as they come."

"He sounds like a fine and sensible lad," said Mr. Blake. "Wouldn't you say so, Sarah?"

"Yes, Father," said Sarah. But her thoughts were very far away.

That night, back at home, Sarah could not sleep. She lay in bed and thought about young Josh Tucker. She had heard many stories about the Indians. Some of them had frightened her. She wondered what she would have done in young Josh's place.

She snuggled closer to Rachel. She closed her eyes and tried to sleep. But strange figures crept into her dreams.

Suddenly, her eyes flew open! *Tap. Tap. Tap.* The sound came from outside. Sarah held her breath and listened. *Tap. Tap. Tap.* She heard it again.

She lay still as a mouse. Her heart
pounded in her chest. She could hear it.
 Then Sarah heard the sound a third
time. *Tap. Tap. Tap.* There could be no
mistake!

Softly, very softly, so as not to awaken
Rachel, she got out of bed. She crept to the
window and peeped out. The moon was a
silver puddle in the night sky. In the woods,
something stirred.

Indians!

One! Two! Three! Four! Five! Sarah
counted the dark shapes. She thought she
saw the tips of their arrows in the moonlight.
She felt weak and frightened.

She started to wake Robert. Then she remembered the miller's words. "Scared is for girls and sissies," he had said.

Well, thought Sarah, I am no sissy! I am as brave as young Josh Tucker! I can take care of myself!

Sarah knew where her father kept his gun. Should she get it? But suppose they are friendly Indians, she thought. Of course, it was a funny time for friendly Indians to come creeping through the woods!

Sarah had to be sure. If she were wrong, her father would not think her fine and sensible. He would not think her brave, like young Josh Tucker. He would think she was a baby! A sissy! Sarah had to know.

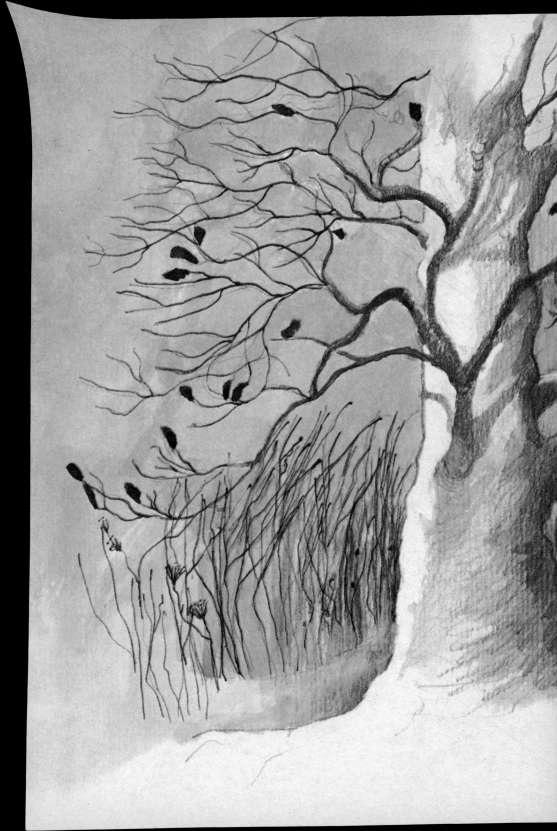

She squinted her eyes. The dark shapes
waved and moved. They swayed in the silver
moonlight. Sarah could not tell if the Indians
carried beads or bows and arrows. Sometimes,
she could not tell if they were there at all.

Very quietly, she slipped out the door. The earth was cool under her bare feet. The night was quiet and still, except for the whisper of a light wind. No dark shapes moved in the woods. Where were the Indians? Were they hiding?

All at once, Sarah remembered. Her window! Her wonderful window! The bumpy glass made the trees *look* alive. There were no Indians … only pine trees that waved and shivered. There was no reason to be afraid after all. Sarah sighed with relief.

Then she heard it again. *Tap. Tap. Tap.*
This time it was closer. Much closer! And
this time there were footsteps. Soft, steady
footsteps. Sarah wanted to cry out.

Suddenly, a hand came down upon her
shoulder.

Her father's voice said: "Sarah! What are you doing out here at this time of night?" He was carrying his gun.

Sarah could hardly speak. She threw her arms around her father. How good his big, strong body felt. How safe! For a long time, Sarah said nothing.

Tap. Tap. Tap. This time they both heard it. "That noise," whispered Sarah. "What is it?"

Her father took Sarah's hand in his own. He took her to where the apple tree grew, just outside her bedroom window. Just then, the autumn breeze stirred its branches. They moved against the glass. *Tap. Tap. Tap.*

"So, that is what it was," breathed
Sarah.

"That is what it was," said her father.
"When I was a young lad, about your age, I
was scared out of my wits by the shadow of
my breeches hanging on a nail. You were
brave to come out alone, Sarah. Very
foolish—but brave."

He put his arm around Sarah's shoulders. The apple tree moved in the gentle breeze. *Tap. Tap. Tap.* Sarah smiled up at her father. Then, together, they went into the house.